Barbie™

MYSTERY FILES #5

The Mystery of the Lost Valentine

Want to read more of Barbie's Mystery Files? Don't miss the first three books in the series, *The Haunted Mansion Mystery*, *The Mystery of the Jeweled Mask*, and *Mystery Unplugged*.

Barbie™
MYSTERY FILES #5

The Mystery of the Lost Valentine

By Linda Williams Aber

SCHOLASTIC INC.

New York   Toronto   London   Auckland   Sydney
Mexico City   New Delhi   Hong Kong   Buenos Aires

ISBN 0-439-55708-9

Designed by Peter Koblish
Photography by Tom Wolfson, Sheryl Fetrick, Greg Roccia,
Lawrence Cassel, Scott Meskill, Judy Tsuno, and Lisa Collins

12 11 10 9 8 7 6 5 4 3 2 1   4 5 6 7 8 9/0

Printed in the U.S.A.
First printing, January 2004

Chapter 1

● ●

A SURPRISE VISIT

"Welcome to Maryville Farm!" Barbie read the sign aloud. "Well, Kira, it looks like we're here!"

"I can't wait to see Aunt Emma's face when we show up at her door!" Kira said. "She'll be so surprised!"

"And happy to see us, I hope!" Barbie laughed.

"Oh, yes," Kira replied. "Valentine's Day is tomorrow. This will be our valentine to Aunt Emma! I think she gets lonely out here in the winter. She'll be glad to have company."

Barbie steered her car up the long winding road. They drove past two young boys in winter jackets. They were handing a pair of binoculars back and forth, watching a hawk flying above them. "They look like twins," Barbie said.

1

"Oh, that must be Brad and Chad Hilton," Kira explained. "They are twins. They visit their uncle at the farm next door. I can't believe how big they are. They must be about ten years old now."

The two boys fought over the binoculars. When one got them, the other chased him, trying to get them back. They both ended up running into an old, run-down barn.

The snow from the week before had melted and the road was clear. "Everything looks just as beautiful as you said it would," Barbie said.

"Oh, but wait!" Kira said with a worried look on her face. "Something doesn't look right at the house. Aunt Emma always keeps the curtains open. Everything is closed! I hope she's here."

"Well," said Barbie, "there's only one way to find out. Let's ring the doorbell." She parked the car in front of the big, old farmhouse. The two friends got out and walked up the steps to the front door.

Dingdong. No answer.

Knock, knock. No answer.

"Aunt Emma?" Kira called through the closed door. "Are you home?"

Barbie saw the curtain move at the window by the door. Someone peeked out. The front door opened just a crack. "Who is it?" a frightened voice called out.

"Aunt Emma! It's me, Kira!" Kira replied.

The door opened slowly. An elderly woman peered through the crack in the door. "Who is it?" the woman asked again.

"Kira!" Barbie's friend replied. "Your niece, Kira, and my friend Barbie."

"Oh, Kira dear!" Aunt Emma cried, opening the door all the way. "Thank goodness it's you! What a wonderful surprise!"

Aunt Emma seemed upset and nervous. Her hair was messy and fell around her face. Her blue eyes looked frightened.

"Come inside quickly!" Aunt Emma said. She stepped back and let the girls in. Then she closed the door and leaned her back against it. "I hope no one followed you," she added.

"Followed us?" Barbie asked.

"Aunt Emma," Kira said, "this is my good friend Barbie."

3

"Oh, yes," Aunt Emma replied. Her eyes brightened. "Kira has told me so much about you. I know you're a newspaper reporter. She also told me you're very good at solving mysteries."

Barbie blushed. "Thank you," she said. "I have solved a few mysteries."

"Ha!" Kira laughed. "She means she's solved a *lot* of mysteries!"

Aunt Emma smiled for the first time since they'd arrived. "Well, then," she said, "I think you're just the person I need to speak with! I hope you're planning to stay for a while."

Kira hugged her aunt. "We were hoping you'd ask us to stay," she said. "We wanted to surprise you."

"You know you and your friends are always welcome at Maryville Farm," Aunt Emma said. "But this time you're more than welcome. I have a mystery that needs solving!"

"A mystery?" Barbie said. "What kind of mystery?"

A worried look crossed Aunt Emma's face. "There have been some very strange things happening here," she said. "I think Maryville Farm is haunted!"

"Haunted?" Barbie and Kira gasped.

"Come in and get settled," Aunt Emma said. "I'll make tea and tell you a story that will make you shiver!"

Chapter 2

· ·

AUNT EMMA'S SHIVERY STORY

Barbie and Kira sat together on Aunt Emma's big, comfy sofa. A fire in the fireplace warmed the old farmhouse. Everything was cozy, but Aunt Emma looked scared as she began her story.

"Oh, girls," Aunt Emma said, "I know you must think I'm acting so strangely. But I'm telling you, there have been some very strange things happening here. I think Maryville Farm has its own ghost!"

"A ghost?" Kira said. "But Aunt Emma, there's no such thing as ghosts! I remember you telling me that when I was a little girl. What's frightened you?"

"Oh, Kira dear," Aunt Emma began, "you are right. I am afraid. For all these years I've lived alone on the farm and felt safe. Now there are things going on here that I can't explain."

"What kinds of things?" Barbie asked. She reached into her tote bag and took out her reporter's notebook. As a reporter for the *Willow Gazette*, Barbie was in the habit of taking notes. "Do you mind if I write down the facts as you tell them?"

"Not at all," Aunt Emma said. "Maybe writing things down will help make everything more clear to me, too."

Kira moved closer to her aunt and held her hand. "Go on with your story, Aunt Emma."

"It all began about a week ago," Aunt Emma said. "I was getting ready for bed. No sooner had my eyes closed than I heard someone calling my name softly. I sat up and listened. 'Emma! Emma!' the voice called to me."

"Oh, Aunt Emma!" Kira gasped. "Who was it?"

"I don't know," Aunt Emma replied. "I was so scared. I turned on the light and looked all around the room. There was no one there!"

"Perhaps you were just starting to dream," Barbie said.

"Or maybe it was just your imagination," Kira added.

Aunt Emma looked at both girls and shook her head. "No," she said, "I wasn't dreaming. I didn't imagine it. Someone or something really was there. Just thinking of that ghostly voice makes me tremble."

"Sometimes the wind can sound like a voice," Barbie said.

"Yes, it can," Aunt Emma agreed. "But the wind doesn't write letters from long ago. The wind doesn't write poems. And the wind doesn't deliver them at all hours of the day and night."

Chapter 3

● ● ● ● ● ● ● ● ● ● ● ● ● ● ● ● ● ● ● ●

A GHOSTLY VOICE

"What letters do you mean, Aunt Emma?" Kira asked.

Aunt Emma reached into the drawer of the table next to the sofa and pulled out a packet of letters. Even before she untied the ribbon around the letters, Barbie and Kira could see that they were quite old. The paper was thin and the handwriting on the outside of the envelopes was old-fashioned.

"May I look at the letters?" Barbie asked.

"Yes, of course," Aunt Emma said. Her hands shook as she handed the letters to Barbie.

"Hmmm," Barbie said as she studied the envelopes. "These stamps are very unusual. They look like stamps made just for collectors."

"Is there a postmark that shows where they were sent from?" Kira asked.

"That's the other interesting thing about the stamps," Barbie replied. "These letters didn't go through any post office. And the stamps are all dated 1953!"

"That means the letters are from more than fifty years ago!" Kira exclaimed.

Aunt Emma shuddered. "Yes!" she cried. "Open one up and you'll see the dates are all from many, many years ago. That's what makes me believe they come from a ghost from the past."

Barbie opened one of the letters. Sure enough, the date in the upper right-hand corner read *February 10, 1953*.

The letter was a short and simple poem written in old-fashioned handwriting. Barbie's sharp reporter's eyes noticed that the ink was the kind used in old-fashioned fountain pens, not ballpoint pens. She read the letter aloud:

> *My darling Emma,*
> *I love you from afar.*
> *My heart is with you*
> *Wherever you are.*
>
> ♥

10

All the letters were love poems and all were signed with a heart. "If it is a ghost," Barbie said, "it's definitely a ghost *writer*! The poems are lovely."

Just as Aunt Emma opened her mouth to answer, a sudden sound stopped her. They all heard it. A soft, ghostly voice whispered, "Emma! Emma! Emma!"

Chapter 4

• • • • • • • • • • • • • • • • • • • •

A CLUE

Barbie jumped up from the sofa and moved quickly to a heating vent in the floor. She pressed her ear against the opening and listened. Only the soft breath of heat blowing filled her ears.

Aunt Emma, Kira, and Barbie stayed quiet and still as they waited to hear the sound again. It wasn't repeated.

"But you did hear it, didn't you?" Aunt Emma asked.

"I did hear something," Kira replied.

"So did I," Barbie agreed. "But the fire started flickering at the same time. That would mean the wind was blowing down the chimney. It could have been the wind playing the same trick on all of us."

Kira agreed. "The chimney flue has to be open

12

when there's a fire burning in the fireplace. Maybe it was just the wind coming down through the chimney. But that still doesn't explain the letters."

"Oh, I just don't want to think about it anymore," Aunt Emma cried. "I want to enjoy my visit with you girls. Let's put the letters and the voices aside and make a good supper."

The girls helped Aunt Emma peel potatoes and carrots. She made them Kira's favorite family recipe, farm stew.

"Aunt Emma won first prize with this stew at the county fair when she was younger than we are," Kira bragged.

"It's delicious!" Barbie said. "I'd love to have the recipe so I can make it again."

"There's a secret ingredient," Aunt Emma said with a smile. "A little salt, a little pepper, and a lot of love. That's what makes a stew taste good!"

Talking about the stew seemed to erase some of the worry lines on Aunt Emma's face. As they worked together to clean up the dishes, Aunt Emma told stories about the old days on the farm.

Kira smiled at Barbie. They both knew that their visit was exactly what Aunt Emma needed.

13

"It's been a long day, Aunt Emma," Kira said. "Do you mind if I turn in early tonight?"

"Not at all, dear," Aunt Emma replied. "In fact, now that you girls are here I might just get a good night's sleep myself!" She started to put the fire out.

"If you don't mind," Barbie said, "I'll do that before I come up. I'm not so tired right now. I'd like to stay here a little longer and just enjoy the fire."

"You do just as you please," Aunt Emma said. "Make yourself comfortable." She led the way upstairs. Kira followed.

Kira stopped before she reached the top step and looked down at Barbie. *Just as I suspected,* Kira thought. Her friend was studying the packet of letters again.

Barbie was already on the case! There was something she noticed about the letters. They all had a distinct smell.

"Sea Spice!" Barbie said aloud. She was holding the letters to her nose. She knew the smell of this men's aftershave very well. Her publisher at the newspaper wore the same scent! *If I follow my nose,* Barbie thought, *I just might find this ghost writer!*

Chapter 5

● ● ● ● ● ● ● ● ● ● ● ● ● ● ● ● ● ● ● ●

THE BROKEN LOCKET

Barbie and Kira awoke to the smell of bacon cooking. Aunt Emma was humming a cheerful tune. The girls joined her in the kitchen. "Good morning!" Kira said.

"Good morning to you!" Aunt Emma said. "And I hope you're hungry. I'm making special pancakes for this special day."

"Heart-shaped pancakes!" Kira exclaimed. "I remember those. You always made them for us on Valentine's Day."

"And that's exactly what today is!" Aunt Emma replied.

"We know," Kira said, smiling. "Happy Valentine's Day from us!" She handed her aunt a big box of chocolates. "Sweets for the sweetest," she added.

Before they had finished breakfast, a loud *clunk*

sounded outside. All three of them jumped. "What was that?" Kira asked.

"Oh, that was just Hank the mailman leaving the mail," Aunt Emma replied. "Would you get that for me, dear?"

"I'll do it," Barbie said. She went to the door and opened it just in time to see the mailman's truck going down the drive. The local paper and a couple of bills were all that was in the mailbox.

As she started to go back inside, a creaking noise around the corner of the house caught her attention. Barbie went to investigate. She found a shutter that had come loose. It was swinging back and forth slightly.

More interesting to Barbie was the cellar door on the ground under the creaking shutter. A rusted lock held the double doors closed. Barbie looked closer. The lock was not completely closed! She pulled one of the doors open and peered down into a dark hole.

"Barbie?" came Kira's voice from the front porch. "Coming!" Barbie called. She would come back later with a flashlight.

When Barbie got back inside, Kira and Aunt

Emma were mixing up cookie dough. Valentine heart cookie cutters were set out. "This is another one of Aunt Emma's traditions," Kira explained. "We always used to make Valentine's Day cookies and decorate them."

"What fun!" Barbie said. She took the apron Kira held out for her. The three women got right into the spirit of the activity.

Soon the kitchen smelled of fresh-baked cookies. The three bakers were so busy they didn't hear another *clunk* outside.

When they were finished baking the last batch, Aunt Emma needed a nap. The girls decided to take a walk. As they stepped onto the porch, Barbie gasped. The mailbox was open and sticking out of it was a large envelope! It had an old three-cent stamp and the same handwriting as on the other letters.

"Oh, dear!" Kira said. "Just when Aunt Emma was feeling so happy again."

"We'd better show it to her," Barbie said, feeling the envelope with her fingers. "There's something more than just a letter inside. It feels like a key, maybe."

17

The girls went on their walk. When they returned, Aunt Emma was awake and refreshed.

"I'm afraid we have something to show you that you won't like," Kira told her.

Barbie held out the envelope to Aunt Emma. The happy expression on the old woman's face disappeared. "Oh, no," she said. "I can't open it. You do it, please."

Barbie carefully opened the envelope. Inside was a large, lacy homemade valentine with a poem written on it. Barbie read it aloud:

> *To Emma*
> *Be My Valentine*
> *If I can have one wish come true,*
> *I know what it will be.*
> *I wish that someday you'll be mine*
> *And that you'll marry me.*
> *If I ask you for your hand,*
> *You may send me away.*
> *So to be safe I'll simply write*
> *Love letters every day.*
> ♥

18

P.S. If you wonder who I am,
This broken heart holds the key.
When you find the other half,
You also will find me!

Barbie reached into the envelope again and pulled out a beautiful silver heart locket on a chain. Only the front part of the locket was there. The back of it was broken off.

"Whoever it is wants to be found, I think," Barbie said. "But the date is from 1953. February fourteenth, 1953. And I know for a fact this didn't come with the regular mail."

"They never do," Aunt Emma said sadly. "They never do."

Chapter 6

• • • • • • • • • • • • • • • • • • • •

MR. SWINDON'S SHOP

"I remember this kind of locket very well," Aunt Emma said. "The engraving looks as if it was done by hand. It's lovely. When I was a young girl it was very fashionable to wear a locket."

Barbie examined it closely. "I can see that it was made to hold a small photograph," she said. "There are hinges where the back of it would connect to the front."

"Yes," Aunt Emma said, "people put pictures of their loved ones in their lockets. Lockets were probably Swindon's bestselling item."

"Hmm," Barbie said. "Didn't we drive past Swindon's Jewelry on our way through town, Kira?"

"Yes, we did," Kira replied.

"Not much has changed in the town," Aunt

Emma said. "Mr. Swindon still runs the store. Of course, he's quite elderly now."

"That gives me an idea!" Barbie said. "If you don't mind, I'd like to borrow that locket and show it to Mr. Swindon. Perhaps he'll be able to tell me something about it."

"I don't mind at all," Aunt Emma said. "The sooner you take it out of this house, the better."

Kira put her arm across Aunt Emma's shoulder. "Everything will be all right," she said. "I'll stay with you while Barbie goes into town."

Barbie slipped the locket and the lacy card back into the envelope. "I'll be back soon," she told Kira and Aunt Emma. "And I hope I'll have some information that will help solve this mystery."

Finding Swindon's Jewelry Store was easy. It was right in the middle of Main Street. Barbie pulled her car into a spot in front of the old store. The windows were dusty and filled with all kinds of things besides jewelry. There were also old toys, clocks and watches, and lots of books. Barbie walked inside the store. There was no one behind the counter. "Hello?" she called out. "Mr. Swindon?"

"Just a minute, miss," a scratchy voice replied from a back room. "I'll be right with you."

As she waited, Barbie looked into a glass case filled with old and new jewelry. Bracelets, rings, and necklaces were in one case. Another case was filled with heart-shaped lockets.

"May I help you?" the scratchy voice asked.

Barbie looked up. She was face-to-face with the elderly Mr. Swindon. "Hello," she said. "I was wondering if you might be able to take a look at a broken locket I have?" She took out the envelope and emptied the locket into her hand.

"Where did you get that, miss?" Mr. Swindon asked. Instead of taking the locket, he took the envelope. "This stamp!" he said. "Where did you get it?"

"I know it's quite old, but . . ." Barbie began.

"This stamp is one of the rarest ever created," Mr. Swindon said. "Many years ago, someone in town collected stamps. I've forgotten his name now. But the strange thing is, you're the second person this week to bring one into my shop!"

"If you happen to think of the name of the person who collected those stamps, would you mind

22

calling me at this number?" Barbie requested, handing the man her business card. She circled her cell phone number.

"Certainly, miss," he said.

"And who was the person who brought you the stamp?" Barbie asked.

"I'm sorry, miss," the shop owner said. "That's confidential. I never talk about customers without their permission. But I can tell you the stamp was traded for an old pair of binoculars."

Barbie's eyes lit up. "Thanks, Mr. Swindon!" she said. "You've been a big help!"

Barbie smiled all the way back to Maryville Farm. Mr. Swindon had given her the best clue so far!

Chapter 7

●●●●●●●●●●●●●●●●●●●●●

THE STORM CELLAR

Barbie returned to the farm just in time to meet the mailman. He was walking up to the front porch. "Good afternoon," he said, tipping his hat to her. He was a kindly-looking man with sad eyes.

"Good afternoon," Barbie replied. "I'll save you the trip up the steps and take the mail for my friend."

"Thank you very much," the mailman said, handing her the mail. "Good day to you now." He got back into his mail truck and drove slowly away.

Barbie sniffed the air. Something familiar caught her attention. It was the scent of Sea Spice after-shave. *Is Hank the mailman delivering the love letters to Aunt Emma?* Barbie wondered.

Barbie started up the steps. The mailbox was partly open. Inside was another letter with an old stamp. Barbie plucked the letter from the box. The scent of Sea Spice was on the letter.

"But how did this letter get here before Hank did?" Barbie asked out loud. Barbie opened the door to the house and went inside.

As she hung up her coat, she heard the soft, ghostly voice coming from nowhere. "Emma! Emma! Emma!"

Quickly, Barbie listened at the vent in the floor. Then she pressed her ear against the wall by the fireplace. A rustling sound seemed to come from under the fireplace floor. "Aha!" Barbie exclaimed, pulling her coat back on. She rushed outside.

Just as she thought, the fireplace was above the cellar doors. The rusty lock was lying on the ground. One door was open. Fresh footprints led to and from the cellar door. Was someone down there now?

Barbie peered into the darkness. "Who's in there?" she called out. No one answered.

Barbie knew it was not safe to go into the cellar without a flashlight. She rushed back inside the house and found one in the kitchen. Then she stepped into the basement. Her shoes sank into

25

the dirt floor. A spiderweb brushed against her cheek. She pointed the flashlight at the ground. Fresh footprints were all around the small room. In one corner there was a large tin box with the top closed.

Her heart was pounding. Barbie picked up the box and opened it. To her surprise, a strong scent of Sea Spice met her nose. The box was filled with letters like the ones Aunt Emma had been receiving! And at the bottom of the box something was shining.

Just as Barbie was about to see what it was, the door to the cellar slammed shut above her! "Hey!" she cried. "Let me out!"

Barbie climbed the steps and pushed against the door. Someone on the other side was pushing back. Barbie used all her strength and pushed again. This time, the door flew open and Barbie came face-to-face with Hank the mailman!

"You!" she cried. The box fell out of her hand and landed open on the ground. Letters spilled out. So did a heart-shaped piece of jewelry.

"You!" the mailman said at the same time. He

26

looked surprised. "Where did you get my letters?" he cried. His face was bright red.

"*Your* letters?" Barbie gasped.

The mailman grabbed the letters and the necklace, turned on his heel, and rushed to his truck.

"Wait! Come back!" Barbie called. But it was no use. The mailman had already pulled the door closed and started the engine.

Chapter 8

· ·

HEART TO HART

Aunt Emma and Kira came outside just in time to block the way of the mail truck. The mailman pulled his truck to the side of the road and got stuck in the ditch!

Barbie ran to the side of the truck.

Aunt Emma and Kira joined her. The mailman got out and looked at the truck wheels stuck in the ditch.

Seconds later, the twin boys, Brad and Chad, came running up to the scene. "We saw what happened through our binoculars!" Chad said.

"Uncle Hank," said Brad, "we'll help push your truck out of the ditch."

The mailman was still red in the face from the surprise of Barbie holding his letters. Now he was embarrassed about getting stuck. He was grateful to be able to get back inside his truck. While he started the engine, the boys pushed until it was free.

Just then, Barbie's cell phone rang. "Hello?" she said. "Yes, Mr. Swindon . . . you remembered his name? Hart? Henry Hart? Very well, thank you so much for calling."

"Why was someone calling you about Uncle Hank?" Brad asked. All eyes turned to the mailman.

Suddenly, Barbie put all the pieces of the puzzle together. "Aunt Emma," she said, "it's getting cold out here. How would you like to invite everyone in for some Valentine's Day cookies and tea?"

Aunt Emma looked surprised, but she trusted Barbie. "Certainly," she said. "Won't you all come in?"

The mailman started to refuse politely. But Aunt Emma just smiled. "Oh, come on now, Hank. Don't be shy. Come in and have one of my famous cookies."

"Yeah, come on, Uncle Hank!" the twins said together.

As soon as Aunt Emma was in the kitchen getting

the cookies, Barbie had an idea. "Brad," she said, "would you mind calling Kira's aunt back into this room? Just call for Emma."

"Sure," Brad said. "Emma!" he called. "Emma!"

Aunt Emma came running from the kitchen. She looked frightened. "Did you hear it? Did you all hear it this time?"

Brad quickly slapped his hand over his mouth. Barbie's trick had worked.

"Aunt Emma," Barbie said, "meet the ghost of Maryville Farm. Or should I say, meet the ghosts?"

Brad and Chad looked down at their feet. Their uncle looked too surprised to speak.

"What's going on, Barbie?" Kira asked.

"I think we should let Brad and Chad tell us all what's going on," Barbie said.

"We didn't mean any harm," Chad began.

"We found the tin box in Uncle Hank's attic," Brad added.

"When we opened it and found the letters, we recognized the name on the envelope," Chad said. "We thought it would be nice for Uncle Hank to finally have the letters delivered. Fifty years is a long time to like someone and not tell them."

"So we took some stamps from his collection and mailed the letters. But then we wanted to buy binoculars so we could see when Uncle Hank was finished delivering mail here," Brad said. "Mr. Swindon told us the stamps were really valuable. So we traded one for the binoculars."

"And when Mr. Swindon called, he told me the name of the person who collected those stamps was Henry Hart," Barbie said. "Each letter was signed with a heart, but that heart really stood for Hart. Am I right, Mr. Hart?" she asked the mailman.

The mailman was blushing. So was Aunt Emma.

"I never knew you even noticed me," Aunt Emma said shyly.

"And I never thought you would notice me," the mailman replied.

"So maybe our plan worked!" Chad exclaimed. "We're sorry we scared you. We didn't want you to think the house was haunted. We just called your name to get your attention, so you would check the mailbox."

"Well," said the mailman, "Emma, would you have dinner with me?"

Aunt Emma picked up the plate of cookies and

passed it to Henry Hart. "I'd love to have dinner with you, Hank," she said, "but only if you'll have this heart."

The mailman took a heart-shaped cookie and smiled. "Heart to Hart," he said. He reached into his pocket and pulled out his wallet. Inside was the other half of the locket—with Emma's picture inside. He handed it to Emma.

Emma gasped. "Heart to Hart indeed," she whispered, smiling. "Happy Valentine's Day, Hank."

"This is one Valentine's Day I think we'll all remember," Barbie said. "The Mystery of the Lost Valentine is solved! Case closed!"

Reporter's Notebook

Can YOU solve *The Mystery of the Lost Valentine*? Read the notes below. Collect more notes of your own. Then YOU solve it!

Assignment: Solve the mystery of the ghostly whispers and the love letters written fifty years ago.

● ●

Background Info:
• Aunt Emma hears her name whispered and no one is there.
• Love letters written fifty years ago arrive before and after regular mail deliveries.
• Barbie and Kira surprise Aunt Emma with a visit and stay to solve the mystery.

Mystery:
Who: Who is the ghost? Who is delivering the letters? Who wrote them?
What: What does the smell of Sea Spice on the letters mean?

How: How are the letters getting into Aunt Emma's mailbox?

Where: Where is the sound coming from?

Why: Why is a ghost haunting Aunt Emma?

Facts and Clues:

- Letters are dated fifty years ago.
- Letters are written with fountain pen, not ball-point pen.
- Stamps are not canceled.
- Stamps are collectors' items.
- Broken locket

Suspects:

- Hank the mailman
- Brad and Chad, the twins
- Mr. Swindon

Additional Notes:

Clue #1 _____
_____
_____
_____
_____

Clue #2 _____
_____
_____
_____
_____

Clue #3 _____
_____
_____
_____
_____

Clue #4 _____
_____
_____
_____
_____

Now YOU Solve It!

_____

_____

_____

_____

_____

_____

_____

_____

_____

_____

_____

_____

_____

_____

_____

_____

_____

_____

_____

_____

_____

_____